Caught in the Act!

"What is the meaning of this?" Mr. Daly pulled a piece of balled-up newspaper out of his desk drawer. Then another. And another.

"Everyone to the front of the room," Mr. Daly ordered. "Make one line facing me."

Mr. Daly stood in front of the class. "Newspaper is dirty," he said. "That means the joker will be the student with the dirtiest hands."

Nancy held out her hands. They looked clean. So did Bess's. But George's hands were dirty.

"I found a worm on our driveway," George whispered to Nancy. "I had to put it back in the ground."

Mr. Daly walked down the row of students. He passed Nancy and Bess quickly. But he studied George's hands for a long time. "The joker is Miss Georgia Fayne!" he announced.

The Nancy Drew Notebooks

1 The Slumber Party Secret
2 The Lost Locket
3 The Secret Santa
4 Bad Day for Ballet
5 The Soccer Shoe Clue
6 The Ice Cream Scoop
7 Trouble at Camp Treehouse
8 The Best Detective
9 The Thanksgiving Surprise
#10 Not Nice on Ice
#11 The Pen Pal Puzzle
#12 The Puppy Problem
#13 The Wedding Gift Goof
#14 The Funny Face Fight
#15 The Crazy Key Clue
#16 The Ski Slope Mystery
#17 Whose Pet Is Best?
#18 The Stolen Unicorn
#19 The Lemonade Raid
#20 Hannah's Secret
#21 Princess on Parade
#22 The Clue in the Glue
#23 Alien in the Classroom
#24 The Hidden Treasures
#25 Dare at the Fair
#26 The Lucky Horseshoes
#27 Trouble Takes the Cake
#28 Thrill on the Hill
#29 Lights! Camera! Clues!
#30 It's No Joke!

Available from MINSTREL Books

THE

NANCY DREW NOTEBOOKS®

#30

It's No Joke!

CAROLYN KEENE
ILLUSTRATED BY JAN NAIMO JONES

Published by POCKET BOOKS
New York London Toronto Sydney Tokyo Singapore

A MINSTREL PAPERBACK *Original*

A Minstrel Book published by
POCKET BOOKS, a division of Simon & Schuster Inc.
1230 Avenue of the Americas, New York, NY 10020

ISBN: 0-671-02493-0

First Minstrel Books printing April 1999

10 9 8 7 6 5 4 3 2 1

Cover art by Joanie Schwarz

Printed in the U.S.A.

QBP/X

It's No Joke!

1

The Substitute

"Look at me!" eight-year-old Nancy Drew said. "I'm a tiger."

Nancy bared her teeth and growled. She held her fingers far apart and pretended her hands were claws.

"I'm a rhinoceros!" George Fayne said.

George held her hands over her nose to make a horn. Then she ran in a circle around Bess Marvin. Nancy chased after her.

"Cut it out, you guys," Bess said. "You're making me dizzy."

Nancy, George, and Bess were on the playground at Carl Sandburg Elementary School. The girls were waiting for school to begin. They were all in the same third-grade class.

Nancy stopped running. "Sorry, Bess," she said. "I'm just excited about our trip to the zoo."

George stopped, too. "It's only four days away now," she added.

Bess's eyes were bright. "I can't wait," she said. "But I don't want to see scary animals like tigers. I want to see the flamingos. They're pretty and pink."

"Okay," George agreed. "We can do that—right after we see the vampire bats. Blah-ha-ha!"

Nancy smiled. Sometimes she had a hard time believing that her two best friends were actually cousins. They were so different.

George was tall and had dark, curly hair. She loved sports. Bess was shorter, had long blond hair, and liked clothes much more than outdoor games. Nancy wasn't surprised that her friends were looking forward to seeing different animals at the zoo.

Brring! The school bell rang. The girls joined the crowd of noisy kids walking into school. Nancy, George, and Bess were all in Mrs. Reynolds's class.

The girls walked into their classroom. But Mrs. Reynolds wasn't there. An elderly man sat at her desk. His thick gray hair was carefully combed back. He wore gold spectacles and a gray suit. His jacket was buttoned all the way up.

"Yuck," George whispered. "We have a substitute."

"And he looks mean," Bess added.

He *did* look mean. He didn't smile when the kids came in. Nancy felt sad. Mrs. Reynolds always smiled—especially on Monday morning.

George quietly slipped into her desk at the front of the row. Nancy and Bess walked back to their side-by-side desks. They didn't laugh or joke around. All of the kids in Mrs. Reynolds's class were being extra well-behaved.

"Good morning, boys and girls," the

2×3=6 3×3=9

substitute said. "My name is Mr. Daly. I'm going to be your teacher while Mrs. Reynolds is away."

Several kids groaned.

Mr. Daly frowned. "Rude behavior will not be permitted in this classroom," he said sternly.

Emily Reeves raised her hand.

"Yes, Miss Reeves?" Mr. Daly said.

Nancy and Bess exchanged looks. *Miss Reeves?* Mr. Daly was so formal. And how had he learned Emily's name so quickly?

"Is Mrs. Reynolds sick?" Emily asked.

"No, she isn't," Mr. Daly said. "Mrs. Reynolds had to go out of town on family business this week."

Nancy gasped. Mrs. Reynolds was going to be out all week? That meant she wouldn't be back in time for the field trip.

"Are we still going to the zoo?" Nancy called out.

Mr. Daly frowned at Nancy. "If you have something to say, Miss Drew, please raise your hand and wait to be called on."

Nancy felt her face grow hot. She slipped down in her seat and wished she could disappear. Everyone was staring at her.

Mike Minelli raised his hand.

"Yes, Mr. Minelli?" Mr. Daly asked.

"Are we still going to the zoo?" Mike demanded.

"Naturally," Mr. Daly said. "I've led hundreds of field trips. One more won't hurt me."

Mr. Daly made taking the class to the zoo sound like a chore. Mrs. Reynolds never did that. She liked field trips almost as much as the kids did.

Going to the zoo won't be as much fun without Mrs. Reynolds, Nancy thought. But she still wanted to go. She was glad Mr. Daly hadn't called off the trip.

Mr. Daly took attendance. Then he told the kids to raise their hands if they had their permission slips to go on the field trip.

Nancy raised her hand. So did Bess and George and lots of other kids.

Mr. Daly began collecting their permission slips.

Nancy looked across the classroom. She saw that Julia Santos didn't have her hand raised.

Uh-oh, Nancy thought.

The week before, Mrs. Reynolds had let the students choose buddies for the field trip. Buddies sat on the bus together, walked around the zoo together, and ate lunch together. Your job was making sure your buddy didn't get lost.

George and Bess were going to be buddies. Julia was going to be buddies with Nancy. Nancy was happy because Julia was lots of fun.

"Julia didn't bring in her permission slip," Bess whispered to Nancy.

"I know," Nancy said. "But I'm sure she'll remember it tomorrow."

Julia loved the zoo just as much as Nancy. The girls had been talking about the trip for weeks. They planned to wear matching red T-shirts. That way everyone would know they were buddies.

Mr. Daly went to the chalkboard. He wrote down a long list of rules. "Please copy these onto a clean sheet of paper," he said. "I expect you to follow these rules for the next week."

Nancy felt like sticking out her tongue. Copying off the board was baby work. Mrs. Reynolds never made them do boring stuff like that.

The kids began writing. Mr. Daly walked up and down the rows. He looked over the kids' shoulders.

Mr. Daly stopped next to Nancy's desk. "Neatness counts," he said.

Nancy bit her lip. She tried to write more neatly. Mrs. Reynolds liked neat papers, too. But she never thought Nancy's were messy.

Mr. Daly continued to walk up and down the rows. He was on the other side of the classroom when Bess poked Nancy.

"Look," Bess whispered.

Nancy looked at Mr. Daly. She laughed out loud. Then she covered her mouth with her hand.

Someone had taped a sign on the substitute's back. The sign said Old Meanie.

2

Mike's Promise

Mr. Daly heard the kids laughing. He found the sign on his back and pulled it off. He balled the sign up and tossed it in the wastebasket.

Mike burst into loud laughter. So did his best friend, Jason Hutchings.

Mr. Daly's face was red. "The jokes will end," he said quietly. "Or I will cancel Friday's trip to the zoo."

Mike and Jason stopped laughing.

Nancy frowned at Bess. Mr. Daly *couldn't* call off the zoo trip. They'd been looking forward to it practically forever.

I have to make sure the joker doesn't cause any more trouble, Nancy decided.

That means I have to figure out who put the sign on Mr. Daly's back.

Nancy quickly came up with a plan. She waited until the class was busy doing a set of math problems. Then she raised her hand.

"Yes, Miss Drew?" Mr. Daly asked.

"May I sharpen my pencil?" Nancy asked.

"Certainly," Mr. Daly said.

Nancy walked to the front of the classroom. She sharpened her pencil. Then—when Mr. Daly wasn't looking—she pulled the sign out of the wastebasket. She slipped the sign into her pocket and hurried back to her desk.

The morning dragged on. The kids finished their math problems. Then they measured the bean plants they were growing for science. Mr. Daly read them a story about a pioneer family.

Finally, the lunch bell rang. Nancy and her friends hurried out of the classroom. They walked toward the lunchroom together.

"I saw you get the sign out of the garbage," George said. "What are you going to do with it?"

"Find out who wrote it," Nancy said. She led the way to one of the lunchroom bulletin boards. Work from Mrs. Reynolds's class was hanging there. Nancy held the sign up to the board.

"See if the writing on the sign matches any of these papers," Nancy said.

"Look!" Bess said after a minute. She pointed to the *M* in *Meanie*. Then she pointed to an *M* on Mike Minelli's paper. The two letters looked exactly the same.

"Mike made the sign," Nancy said.

"What a surprise!" George rolled her eyes and laughed. Mike and his friends were famous for playing jokes.

"Let's go talk to him," Bess said.

The girls marched over to the table where Mike and Jason were eating.

Jason made a face when he saw them coming. "Girl alert! Girl alert!" he said.

"No girls allowed at this table," Mike added.

"We'll leave as soon as we finish talking to you," George said.

Mike made a face. "Then hurry up and talk," he said.

"We know you stuck that sign on Mr. Daly's back," Nancy told him.

"So?" Mike asked. "What are you going to do? Tell on me?"

"No," George said. "We just want you to stop."

"Please don't mess up our field trip," Bess added.

Mike sighed. "Don't worry," he said. "I want to see the alligators at the zoo. I'm planning to be good for the rest of the week. Even if Mr. Daly *is* an old meanie."

Nancy smiled at Mike. "Thanks," she said. She was glad that Mike wanted to go to the zoo as much as she did. Now she didn't have anything to worry about.

* * *

Tuesday morning was rainy. Nancy's father gave her a ride to school. When they got there, the playground was empty. Nancy went straight inside. Her classroom was already full of kids.

George and Bess were talking to Julia. Julia had a towel around her shoulders. Her dark hair was damp. So was the front of her T-shirt.

Nancy walked over to her friends. "What happened to you?" she asked Julia.

"I got soaked walking to school," Julia explained. "The school nurse gave me this towel."

"Why didn't you get a ride?" Bess asked.

"Dad was at work," Julia said. "And Mom had a doctor's appointment this morning."

"You should have taken the school bus," Bess said. "That's what I did."

George shrugged. "Getting a little wet is no big deal," she said. "Right, Julia?"

"Um—right," Julia agreed.

ate
eight
great

Nancy had other things on her mind. "Did you bring your permission slip in today?" she asked Julia.

Julia got a funny look on her face. "Sorry," she said. "I forgot again."

Nancy frowned at Julia. She didn't understand why her buddy kept forgetting her permission slip. Bringing it in was important.

"Try to remember tomorrow," Nancy told Julia.

"I will," Julia said. "Promise."

"Okay," Nancy said with a smile.

The bell rang and the kids sat down. Mr. Daly walked to the teacher's desk and opened a drawer. Nancy saw his eyes get big.

"What is the meaning of this?" Mr. Daly demanded. He pulled a piece of balled-up newspaper out of his desk drawer. Then another. And another.

Some of the kids started to giggle. Someone had pulled another joke on the substitute!

Mr. Daly opened another desk drawer.

That one was full of balled-up newspaper, too. So was the drawer under that one.

I bet Mike did this, Nancy thought. And he promised not to play any more jokes.

Nancy looked over at Mike's desk. But it was empty. Mike wasn't at school that day. Now Nancy was confused. If Mike didn't play the joke, who did?

"Everyone to the front of the room," Mr. Daly ordered. "Make one line facing me."

Nancy got in line between George and Bess.

Mr. Daly stood in front of the class. "Newspaper is dirty," he said. "That means the joker will be easy to catch. He or she will be the child with the dirtiest hands. Hold out your hands, please."

Nancy held out her hands. They looked clean. So did Bess's. But George's hands were dirty.

"Have you been digging in the mud?" Nancy whispered to George.

George nodded. "I found a worm on our driveway," she whispered. "I had to put it back in the ground."

Nancy held her breath as Mr. Daly walked down the row of students. He passed Nancy and Bess. But he studied George's hands for a long time. Then he walked quickly to the end of the line.

Mr. Daly turned to the kids. "The joker is Miss Georgia Fayne!" he announced.

3

Bess and the Goldfish

Georgia?

A moment passed before Nancy realized Mr. Daly was talking about George. Nobody called her by her real name. She didn't like it.

"Everyone except Miss Fayne may sit down now," Mr. Daly said.

Nancy and Bess gave George sad looks. They walked back to their seats. So did the rest of the class.

George stood in front of the class. Her face was red. She looked angry.

Nancy was angry, too. Mr. Daly was blaming George for something she hadn't done. That wasn't fair.

"Miss Fayne, please clean the newspaper out of my desk," Mr. Daly said.

George stomped over to the teacher's desk. She began pulling newspaper out of the drawers. She tossed the balled-up pages into the wastebasket.

Mr. Daly faced the class. "Miss Fayne will stay at school on Friday while the rest of us go to the zoo," he announced. "I do not take jokers on field trips."

George's mouth dropped open. She looked even more upset. "But I didn't do anything!" she said.

Mr. Daly pretended not to hear George.

He is so mean, Nancy thought. She wished she could tell him that George wasn't guilty. But she knew the substitute wouldn't believe her.

George finished cleaning out Mr. Daly's desk. She went back to her seat.

Mr. Daly did math, then science, then history. Once again the morning seemed to stretch on and on. When the lunch bell finally rang, Nancy jumped out of her seat. She ran to talk to George and Bess.

"I can't believe you're not going to the zoo with us," Bess said.

"*I* can't believe he thinks I put that newspaper in his desk," George said.

"I wonder who really did it," Nancy said.

"I have a clue," George whispered. "I'll show it to you in the lunchroom."

A few minutes later, the girls sat down at their favorite table. They unwrapped their lunches. Then George pulled a piece of newspaper out of her pocket.

"Where did you get that?" Nancy asked.

"Out of Mr. Daly's desk," George said. "Most of the newspaper I cleaned out looked normal. But this piece is different. I think it's written in a foreign language."

George put the paper on the table. The girls leaned over it. Nancy didn't recognize any of the words.

"What language is it?" Bess asked.

"I don't know," Nancy said.

Rebecca Ramirez came up to their

table. She lived near Nancy. The two girls often walked to school together. Rebecca wanted to be an actress when she grew up. She made a big drama out of everything.

"Scoot over quick!" Rebecca said. "I'm going to faint if I don't eat soon."

"Sure," Nancy said with a smile. She moved over to make room for her friend.

Rebecca sat down and took out her food. But before she took a bite, she noticed the newspaper. "What are you guys doing?" she asked.

"Trying to figure out what language this is written in," George said. She explained about the zoo trip and the joker.

Rebecca looked at the paper. "It's Spanish," she said. "I know because I'm taking Spanish lessons after school."

"Can you read what it says?" Nancy asked.

Rebecca studied the paper for a long time. Then she shook her head. "I've only been studying Spanish a few

months," she said. "This doesn't make any sense to me."

"Too bad," Nancy said.

"I have an idea, though," Rebecca added. "You could show this to Abuela."

"Who?" Nancy asked.

Rebecca smiled. "Abuela," she repeated. "That means grandmother in Spanish. My abuela reads a Spanish newspaper every day. Reading this will be easy for her."

George looked excited. "When will you see your grandmother?" she asked Rebecca.

"She comes to our house every Wednesday after school," Rebecca explained. "You could show her the newspaper tomorrow."

"Thanks, Rebecca,!" George said. She put the paper in her lunchbox. "I hope we can find the joker before Friday," she added.

Bess nodded. "The zoo won't be any fun without you."

"*If* we go," Nancy said.

Bess turned to Nancy. "What do you mean?" she asked.

"Well, the joker is still on the loose," Nancy said. "He— "

"Or she," George put in.

Nancy nodded. "He or she could play another joke. And that might make Mr. Daly mad enough to make us all stay at school."

"We can't let that happen," Bess said.

"I know," Nancy agreed. "We have to find a way for the whole class to go to the zoo. Including George."

"Oh, no," Bess whispered the next afternoon.

Nancy looked up from her work. She was practicing her cursive *Q*'s. Mr. Daly was walking around and looking at the students' papers.

"What?" Nancy whispered.

Bess pointed at the teacher's desk.

Nancy looked at it. She saw stacks of papers, the attendance book, and a glass of water.

Then Nancy saw what was worrying Bess. A small bright orange goldfish was swimming around in Mr. Daly's water! The fish was plastic. Another practical joke!

"Mr. Daly is going to be mad when he finds that," Nancy whispered. "I bet he makes us all stay in school and miss the zoo."

Bess got a determined look on her face. "Then we can't let him find it," she whispered. "I'm not missing the flamingos because of some dumb fish."

Before Nancy could answer, Bess got out of her seat. She tiptoed toward Mr. Daly's desk.

Nancy held her breath. Bess was taking a big chance. Mr. Daly would be angry if he caught her out of her seat.

Bess reached the teacher's desk. She carefully picked up the glass of water.

Nancy turned around. Mr. Daly was in the back of the classroom. He was looking at Brenda Carlton's paper. Maybe—just maybe—he wouldn't see what Bess was doing. Nancy crossed her fingers for good luck.

Bess began carrying the water toward the sink.

She's almost there, Nancy thought.

Bess got to the sink. She dumped out the water. She picked up the plastic fish.

Nancy heard footsteps coming up the row of desks. She spun around. Mr. Daly was walking toward the sink. He was looking right at Bess. A big frown made his face look ugly.

"Just what do you think you're doing?" Mr. Daly demanded.

4

Grandma Ramirez

"I—" Bess's eyes were wide. She looked terrified. Everyone in the classroom was staring at her.

"Well, Miss Marvin?" Mr. Daly said. "What are you doing out of your seat?"

"I was, um—" Bess looked confused.

Nancy *had* to do something to help. She noticed the small drinking fountain that was attached to the side of the sink.

"Bess was getting a drink of water," Nancy told Mr. Daly. "Mrs. Reynolds lets us use the drinking fountain whenever we want."

Mr. Daly turned and looked at Nancy.

Then he turned back to Bess. "Is that true, Miss Marvin?"

"I—I guess so," Bess said.

"Then what is that in your hand?" Mr. Daly pointed at the plastic fish.

Bess looked down at it. "Well, it's a fish," she told Mr. Daly.

"A fish you were planning to put in my drinking glass!" Mr. Daly said loudly. "You were going to play another joke on me, weren't you?"

Bess shook her head.

Mr. Daly didn't seem to notice. "Class, Miss Marvin will also stay at school while we go to the zoo on Friday," he announced. "As I said before, I don't take jokers on field trips. Miss Marvin, you may sit down now."

Bess walked back to her desk. Nancy could see tears welling up in her friend's eyes. She felt awful. Bess had only been trying to help. She didn't deserve to miss the trip.

Nancy felt sorry for herself, too.

Going to the zoo wouldn't be as much fun without Bess and George.

Mr. Daly collected the handwriting exercise. He gave the class their spelling words. They were supposed to write a sentence with each one.

Nancy was one of the first students to finish. Mr. Daly said she could have some free time.

Great, Nancy thought. Now I can work on figuring out who the real joker is!

Nancy pulled her detective notebook out of her desk. Her father had given it to her. The notebook's shiny cover was Nancy's favorite color—blue. Inside, she kept notes on all of her mysteries.

Nancy turned to a clean page. Then she wrote: "The Case of the Practical Jokes." Under that, she wrote: "Clues: Newspaper in Spanish." She skipped a few lines and wrote: "Suspects."

Nancy tapped her pencil against her notebook. She couldn't think of *any* suspects. As far as she knew, nobody in her class spoke Spanish. That was going to make solving this mystery difficult.

"The joker could be anyone in our class," Nancy told George and Bess after school. "We don't have any real suspects."

"But we do have a new clue," Bess said. "The fish."

"The fish?" George asked.

Bess nodded. "I think the School Bell sells plastic fish like the one I found in Mr. Daly's water," she said. "Maybe Mr. Pitt can remember if anyone in our class bought one."

"Good thinking!" Nancy said.

The School Bell was a shop near the school. Charlie Pitt was the shop's owner. He'd opened the School Bell way back when Nancy's father went to Carl Sandburg Elementary. The shop was crammed full of candy, notebooks, pencils, and other supplies. Nancy loved the place.

Bess led the way into the store. The

bell attached to the door jangled. Mr. Pitt looked up and smiled. He had light brown hair and blue eyes. He wore glasses.

"Good afternoon, girls," he said. "How was school today?"

"Rotten," Nancy said. "We have a substitute teacher."

"And he thinks I played a practical joke on him," Bess added.

"I'm sorry to hear that," Mr. Pitt said.

"You guys—look!" George said with a gasp. She pointed at a bowl next to the cash register. The bowl was filled with plastic fish. Every one of them looked just like the fish from Mr. Daly's water.

"Mr. Pitt," Nancy said, "we have to know the name of everyone who bought one of these fish. If we don't find out, Bess and George won't be able to go on our field trip to the zoo."

"That sounds important," Mr. Pitt said. He rubbed his chin thoughtfully. "Let me think. Lots of kids have bought those. They're really great in water."

"We need names," Nancy said.

Mr. Pitt laughed. "Well, I can't remember them all. I've sold about a hundred of those fish."

"A hundred?" Nancy groaned. Having no suspects was bad. Having a hundred suspects would be even worse!

"Can you remember if any of the kids in our class bought one?" Nancy asked.

"Maybe," Mr. Pitt said. "You're in Mrs. Apple's class, right?"

"No," George said. "Mrs. Reynolds's."

"Oh. Right." Mr. Pitt screwed up his face and thought hard. "I'm pretty sure that Danielle Margolies bought one of those."

"Danielle isn't in our class," Bess said.

Mr. Pitt sighed. "Sorry, kids. I don't think I can help you."

George and Bess looked sad.

"I guess we're not going to the zoo now," George said.

"Don't give up," Nancy said. "We still have one more clue. Let's go over to Rebecca's. We can show her grandmother the newspaper."

Before leaving the store, the girls each bought a lollipop. Nancy's tasted like strawberries. They walked over to Rebecca's house and rang the bell.

Rebecca answered the door. "Where have you guys been?" she asked. "My abuela and I have been waiting for *hours!*"

Nancy laughed. "School has only been out for about twenty minutes," she said.

"Well, it *seemed* like hours," Rebecca told her. "I can't wait to see what the newspaper says. Come in. Abuela is in the kitchen."

Rebecca's grandmother was sitting at the kitchen table, reading a cookbook. She was a tiny woman. Her gray hair was cut in a pretty, short style. She had dark, intelligent eyes.

"Abuela, these are the friends I told you about," Rebecca said.

"Hello, girls," Mrs. Ramirez said. "I understand you want me to read something for you."

"Yes, please," George said. She got the newspaper out of her lunchbox.

Rebecca's grandmother smoothed the paper out on the kitchen table. She leaned close and studied it. Then she leaned back with a surprised look on her face.

"What does it say?" Nancy asked.

"I don't know," Rebecca's grandmother told them. "This isn't written in Spanish!"

5

Missing Permission Slip

Nancy and her friends exchanged surprised looks.

"If it's not Spanish, then what is it?" George asked.

Rebecca's grandmother frowned at the newspaper. Then she slowly shook her head. "I'm not sure," she said. "But it may be Portuguese."

"Are you sure you can't read it?" Nancy asked. "Even just a few words might help us."

Rebecca's grandmother studied the paper for another moment. "I think I see the word for 'blue.' "

Blue? Nancy thought. That wasn't much of a clue.

"Anything else?" George asked Rebecca's grandmother.

Mrs. Ramirez pointed at the paper. "This word might mean 'tired.' "

"Tired and blue," Bess said. "That doesn't give us much to go on."

Rebecca's grandmother sighed. "I'm sorry I couldn't help more."

George's shoulders slumped. "Thanks for trying," she told Rebecca's grandmother. She took the piece of newspaper, folded it up, and put it back in her lunchbox.

"Good luck, girls," Rebecca's grandmother said. She turned back to her cookbook.

Rebecca walked with Nancy, Bess, and George to the door. "What are you going to do now?" she asked.

"Give up," George said sadly. "I'm sure we won't figure out who the joker is before Friday morning. And after that, it won't really matter."

"I'm not giving up," Nancy said

firmly. "I'm going to keep looking until I find out who's behind the jokes."

Bess shrugged. "Forget it, Nancy," she said. "Just go to the zoo and have some fun for us."

"No," Nancy said. "I want us all to go to the zoo together. We can solve this mystery if we all work together. Please don't give up now."

"Well . . . okay," George said.

Bess shrugged and nodded.

"Great," Nancy said. She hated to give up.

The girls said goodbye. George and Bess headed home. Nancy walked to her own house.

Hannah Gruen was waiting for her. Hannah had lived with the Drews ever since Nancy's mother died, five years earlier. She seemed like part of the family now.

Hannah made Nancy a peanut butter and jelly sandwich. While she ate, Nancy studied her detective notebook.

She *still* couldn't think of any suspects.

"Do you have a new case?" Hannah asked.

"Yes," Nancy said. "And I only have one more day to solve it!"

"Why is that?" Hannah screwed the top back on the peanut butter.

Nancy told her about the joker. She explained how George and Bess were in trouble with Mr. Daly.

"I don't understand why the joker doesn't stop," Nancy said. "Mr. Daly is thinking about calling off the trip!"

"Maybe that's what the joker wants," Hannah said.

"That doesn't make sense," Nancy told her. "Everyone wants to go to the zoo. At least, I *think* they do."

"I'm still missing two permission slips," Mr. Daly said the next morning. "Miss Santos and Mr. Leoni, did you bring yours today?"

"I have mine!" Andrew announced. He waved the paper over his head.

"Sorry," Julia said quietly. "I forgot again."

Nancy shot her buddy a worried look. The field trip was tomorrow! How could Julia keep forgetting her permission slip? Everyone else in the class had remembered.

"I'll bring it tomorrow," Julia told Mr. Daly. "I promise." She gave Nancy a reassuring smile.

"Okay, Miss Santos," Mr. Daly said. "But if you forget, I'll have to leave you at school. Do you understand?"

Julia nodded.

Nancy sighed as she opened her math book. It was bad enough that George and Bess were missing the field trip. Now it was beginning to look as if Julia wouldn't be coming either. That meant Nancy wouldn't have a buddy.

"What are you going to do if Julia forgets again tomorrow?" Bess whispered to Nancy.

Nancy shrugged. "I don't know."

Bess's eyes widened. "What if you

have to be Mr. Daly's buddy?" she asked.

Nancy made a face. Compared to that, staying at school sounded almost fun. Unless she could find the real joker, this was going to be the worst field trip ever.

That afternoon Nancy brought her detective notebook to lunch with her. "Think!" she told George and Bess. "There must be some clue we've missed."

The girls were quiet for a moment. Nancy stared across the lunchroom. Julia was eating with Emily Reeves and Phoebe Archer a few tables away. They were laughing.

"Maybe we can find someone who reads Portuguese," George suggested.

"That's a good idea," Nancy said. "Like who?"

George shrugged. "Maybe my mom or dad knows someone."

"Okay," Nancy said. "Why don't you ask them after school?"

"Sure," George agreed.

"I'll ask my dad, too," Nancy said.

Emily suddenly jumped out of her chair. Julia got up, too. The two girls raced toward the milk line.

"Walk!" called Mrs. Apple. She was on lunchroom duty.

Emily and Julia immediately slowed down.

Phoebe was still sitting at their table. Nancy turned to smile at her. That was when she noticed Julia's lunchbox. Nobody else in the whole school had a lunchbox like Julia's. It was bright pink with an orange handle.

Julia's lunchbox was sitting open on the table. Nancy could see a piece of paper sticking out. Something about that paper was very familiar.

Nancy got up and started walking toward Julia's table.

"Where are you going?" Bess called.

"I think I just found an important clue," Nancy said. She walked up to Julia's lunchbox and pulled out the paper.

"Hey!" Phoebe said. "What are you doing?"

Bess and George came up behind Nancy. "What did you find?" Bess asked.

Nancy held the paper out to her friends. "Julia's permission slip. And it's already been signed!"

6

Against the Rules

"I don't get it," George said. "Why didn't Julia turn in her permission slip?"

"Maybe she forgot it was in her lunchbox," Bess suggested.

Nancy put the permission slip back where she'd found it. "I don't think Julia forgot," she said. "She would have seen the slip just now when she got her lunch out."

"Then why didn't she give the slip to Mr. Daly?" Phoebe asked. "He told her she couldn't go to the zoo unless he had it."

"I'm not sure," Nancy said. "But I think she was hiding it."

"But hiding the slip doesn't make any sense," George said.

"It might," Nancy said, "if you don't want to go to the zoo."

"But Julia *does* want to go," Bess said. "She told us she wanted to see the polar bears."

"And she told me she wanted to see the zebras," George added.

"I don't understand it either," Nancy said. "But I'm sure Julia will explain."

Emily came back to the table. Julia wasn't with her.

"Where's Julia?" Nancy asked.

"She went to the bathroom," Emily said.

Nancy looked at the clock. Lunch would end in fifteen minutes. "Come on, you guys," she said to Bess and George. "We have to find Julia."

"Where are we going?" George asked.

"To the bathroom," Nancy said.

The girls hurried to the bathroom. Julia wasn't there. They went back to the lunchroom. But Phoebe and Emily and Julia's table was empty. Nancy, Bess, and George went out to the playground. But Julia wasn't playing hopscotch or dodgeball.

"Julia disappeared!" Bess said.

"Now what?" George asked.

Nancy thought for a minute. "We have to go to the classroom right away," she said.

"But that's against the rules," Bess said. "'Stay Out of the Classroom During Lunch Period' was rule number four on the list Mr. Daly made us copy."

"We *have* to go," Nancy said. "It's the only way we can solve the mystery before the field trip."

"Let's go," George said.

Bess groaned. "Oh, all right," she agreed.

Nancy led the way. George and Bess were right behind her. The hallway was empty. The three girls walked quickly to the classroom.

George tried the door. "It's open," she whispered.

The girls walked inside. The room was empty. Mr. Daly had turned the lights out. Nancy felt funny sneaking around in the dark.

"Let's do this fast and get out of here," Nancy whispered.

"Do what?" George whispered.

"Look something up in the big dictionary," Nancy said. She hurried back to the classroom library.

Bess groaned. "We're breaking the rules for *that?"* she asked. "You could have used the dictionary when we got back to class."

"If Mr. Daly let me," Nancy said. "And if he didn't, I would have had to wait and use the dictionary at home. By then it would have been too late to solve the mystery before the field trip. I didn't want to take that chance."

George nodded. "We've got to solve this mystery *now."*

The classroom dictionary stood in the

back of the room. The enormous book had its own wooden stand. Nancy opened the dictionary to the *P*'s. She began flipping through the pages.

"What are you looking for?" George asked.

"The word *Portuguese*," Nancy said. "And here it is." She read silently for a moment. "Listen to this! 'Portuguese. A person who was born in or is a citizen of Portugal.' "

"So what?" George asked. "Nobody in our class is Portuguese. That doesn't help us at all."

"Wait," Nancy said. "There's another definition. 'Portuguese. The language of Portugal *or Brazil*.' "

"They speak Portuguese in Brazil?" Bess asked.

Nancy nodded.

"Julia's mom is from Brazil," George said.

"I know," Nancy said. "And I bet that newspaper belonged to her. Now I'm sure Julia is the joker."

"Let's try to find her," Bess said with excitement. "Maybe she can explain what's going on."

"Good idea!" Nancy closed the dictionary. The girls hurried toward the door. George was about to open it when it swung open.

Mr. Daly walked in. He was carrying a lunch tray. He looked surprised to see the girls.

"What do you think you're doing in here?" Mr. Daly demanded.

George and Nancy and Bess looked at one another. This time Mr. Daly wasn't blaming them for something they hadn't done. This time they'd really broken the rules. Nancy knew she had to tell him the truth.

"We came in to use the dictionary," Nancy said.

"You're not allowed to come into the classroom during lunch," Mr. Daly said.

"I know," Nancy said. "And I'm sorry. But it was very important that we use the dictionary *now*."

"Are you going to explain why?" Mr. Daly asked.

Nancy swallowed hard. She was certain that Julia was the joker. But she couldn't tell Mr. Daly that. Tattling on a friend was wrong. And Nancy was certain that Julia had a good reason for playing the jokes.

"I can't," Nancy told him.

Mr. Daly put his tray down on the desk. He looked angry. "I think I know the reason you sneaked in here," he said. "All three of you have been playing jokes on me. And now you're planting another one."

Nancy shook her head hard. "That's not true," she said.

Nancy's heart was beating double time. Now she knew how George and Bess felt when Mr. Daly accused them of something they hadn't done—awful!

"But—but look around," Nancy said. "We didn't touch anything except for the dictionary."

"We didn't put the newspaper in your desk, either," George said.

"Or put the goldfish in your water," Bess added.

Mr. Daly seemed to be considering what they were saying. He sat down in his desk chair to think. *Pop! Pop, pop, pop!* A bunch of tiny explosions went off under Mr. Daly's chair!

7

Buddies

Mr. Daly pushed himself away from his desk.

Pop! Pop, pop, pop! A second set of little explosions went off under Mr. Daly's chair. His eyes were wide with surprise. He jumped up and stood staring at the chair.

"What was that?" George asked.

"You tell me!" Mr. Daly said.

Nancy crept closer to the chair.

"Be careful," Bess said.

"Don't worry," Nancy said. She looked at the chair seat. Nothing unusual there. She knelt down and peered under the chair. Again, she didn't see anything strange.

Nancy noticed that the chair was sitting on a plastic mat. The mat protected the floor.

"I think there's something under this mat," Nancy said. She held her breath and carefully pushed the chair onto the floor. Nothing happened.

Nancy started to pull up the mat.

But Mr. Daly stepped forward. "I'll do that," he said.

Nancy got out of the way.

Mr. Daly pulled back the plastic.

Nancy let out her breath when she saw what was underneath.

"Look!" Nancy said. "Someone put bubble wrap under the mat. It popped when the chair rolled over it."

"Someone?" Mr. Daly's face was red with anger. "Not just someone—you!"

"It wasn't me," Nancy said.

"Then how did you find the bubble wrap so easily?" Mr. Daly said.

"I—well, I just looked," Nancy said.

"Nancy's good at finding things," Bess added.

"So am I," Mr. Daly said. "And I believe I just found the third joker in this classroom. Miss Drew, you will stay at school tomorrow while the rest of the class goes to the zoo."

Nancy's jaw dropped. She couldn't believe her plan had backfired. She'd tried to fix things so that all of her friends could go to the zoo. Now none of them were going.

A sound startled Nancy. She looked up. The door to the supply closet was opening. Nancy gasped when she saw Julia step out.

"Miss Santos!" Mr. Daly said. "What were you doing in the closet?"

"Hiding," Julia said.

"So, there are actually *four* practical jokers in this classroom," Mr. Daly said.

"No," Julia said. "Nancy didn't put that bubble wrap under your chair. And George and Bess didn't have anything to do with the jokes, either. I played all of them myself."

"Why?" Nancy said.

"And why didn't you say something earlier?" Bess demanded. "It wasn't nice of you to let us take the blame for something you did."

Julia hung her head. "I know," she said. "But I couldn't help myself."

"Why not?" George sounded mad.

Julia looked up at her friends. "I'm afraid to go on the field trip," she whispered.

"You're afraid of the zoo?" Bess asked.

"No," Julia said. "I'm afraid of the school bus."

Julia was talking very softly. Nancy and the others crept closer so that they could hear her.

"Why would you be afraid of the school bus?" Mr. Daly asked.

"Last year something terrible happened," Julia said. "My class went on a trip to a farm. On the way home, I started to feel sick. I thought I could make it back to school. But I was wrong. I threw up all over the bus."

"Gross," Bess said.

Julia nodded without smiling.

George snapped her fingers. "Is that why you walked to school in the rain on Tuesday?" she asked.

"Yes," Julia said. "For me, getting soaking wet is fun compared to riding a bus."

"I don't understand," Nancy said. "We've been on a couple of field trips this year. We've taken the bus both times. And you've never gotten sick."

"That's because Mrs. Reynolds helped me," Julia said. "I told her about my accident at the beginning of the year. She always sits next to me on the bus."

"What does she do?" Nancy asked.

Julia shrugged. "Just talks to me," she said. "Sometimes she tells me jokes. Sometimes she holds my hand. She helps me relax. I can't ride a bus without her. That's why I was trying to get the trip to the zoo called off."

An image popped into Nancy's mind. She could see herself sitting on the school bus next to Julia. They were laughing and talking. Nancy was sad that they weren't going to go to the zoo together.

"Wait!" Nancy said suddenly. "I have an idea. What if *I* help you get over your fear? I can talk and make jokes just the way Mrs. Reynolds usually does."

"Are you sure?" Bess whispered to Nancy. "If your plan doesn't work, Julia might throw up all over you."

Nancy swallowed hard. Bess made helping Julia sound like a bad idea. But Nancy couldn't change her mind now. She didn't want to hurt Julia's feelings.

"I'm sure," Nancy said. "I'm willing to try it if Julia is."

Julia looked worried. She thought about it for a long moment. But then she smiled a little smile. "Okay," she agreed. "I guess that's what buddies are for."

"You guys," George said quietly. "Aren't you forgetting something?"

"What?" Nancy asked.

George tilted her head toward Mr. Daly. He was still standing there with his arms crossed. He still looked angry.

"Three of us aren't *allowed* to go to the zoo," George said. "Remember?"

Nancy turned to Mr. Daly. "Please let us go," she said. "Julia didn't mean to hurt anyone with her practical jokes."

"And I wasn't the one who put that sign on your back," Julia added. "I didn't get the idea to play jokes until after I saw that."

"Pretty please," George said.

"With a cherry and sprinkles," Bess added.

Mr. Daly frowned at them. "Well, I understand why Julia pulled those tricks. But you girls still broke the rules. You sneaked into the classroom during lunch. And that is not allowed."

"Punish us some other way," Nancy suggested. "But please let us go to the zoo."

Mr. Daly scratched his chin. "Well, I don't know . . ." he said.

8

A Frog on the Bus

"Yippee!" George hollered. "The day of our super zoo trip is finally here!"

It was the next morning. Mrs. Reynolds's class was lining up in front of the school.

Mr. Daly had decided to let the entire class go to the zoo—including George, Bess, and Nancy. The girls had gotten their punishment the day before. Mr. Daly had asked them to wash the chalkboard and clean the erasers. Julia had turned in her permission slip.

Nancy and Julia were wearing matching red T-shirts just as they'd planned. Bess and George were standing behind them in line.

All the kids were wearing name tags. Bess's and George's name tags were rabbit-shaped. Nancy's and Julia's were in the shape of lions. Nancy hoped Julia's lion name tag would help her feel brave about riding the bus.

"I'm so excited!" Bess said.

"Me, too," George said.

Nancy felt more nervous than excited. She kept glancing at Julia.

The big yellow school bus was parked right in front of the school. Julia was staring at it. She hadn't said one word for the past five minutes. That was when the bus had arrived.

Nancy was beginning to think riding the bus with Julia wasn't such a good idea. But it was too late to turn back now. Nancy tried not to think of the worst that could happen.

The bus doors opened.

"All aboard!" Mr. Daly called. He was wearing his usual gray suit. But he had added a bright green fishing cap.

"Are you ready?" Nancy asked Julia.

Julia smiled bravely. "Ready," she said.

"Great," Nancy said. She took Julia's hand. They marched up to the bus together. They climbed the steps, walked down the aisle, and picked a seat near the middle. Bess and George sat on the other side of the aisle.

"Okay so far?" Nancy asked Julia.

Julia nodded. "I'm okay," she said. "But we haven't even started moving yet."

"Well, let me know if you begin to feel sick," Nancy said.

"Okay," Julia whispered. She leaned back and closed her eyes.

Mr. Daly counted the kids. Then he sat down. The driver closed the bus door and started up the engine. He pulled away from the school with a lurch.

"We're on our way!" Bess said happily.

"Here we come, zoo!" George added.

Julia didn't smile. She didn't even open her eyes.

Nancy wanted to help Julia relax. She

started to tell her a funny story about her puppy, Chocolate Chip. Halfway through the story, Julia's eyes popped open. She looked scared.

"Are you okay?" Nancy asked.

Julia slowly shook her head. "I think I might be sick."

"I'll get Mr. Daly," Nancy said quickly.

But there wasn't time for that. Julia suddenly leaned forward. She covered her mouth with her hand.

"Mr. Daly!" Nancy shouted toward the front of the bus. "We need your help back here."

"Come quick!" Bess added.

But Mr. Daly didn't seem to hear them. Nancy saw him look quickly up at the roof of the bus.

Mr. Daly got to his feet and turned to the kids. "Who let a frog loose on this bus?" he demanded.

"A frog?" Bess's eyes went wide. She pulled her feet up onto her seat.

Julia sat up. "I didn't do it," she said. "I promise."

"Poor frog," George said. "I bet it's scared half to death."

"If that frog hops on your lap, grab it!" Mr. Daly said. "I'll buy an ice cream for any kid who catches that frog."

Everyone started looking under their seat. Nancy and Julia peeked under theirs, too.

"Do you see it?" Julia asked.

"All I see are a bunch of feet," Nancy said.

"There it is!" Mike hollered. He was sitting near the back of the bus. But he was pointing right at Bess.

"Where?" Bess asked. She sounded afraid.

"Don't worry," George said. *"I'll* catch it!"

"Not if I catch it first!" Julia said. She leaned way out of her seat and looked down the aisle.

Things got pretty noisy. But Mr. Daly didn't try to quiet the kids down. He just made sure that everyone stayed in their seats.

EMERGENCY DOOR

A few minutes later, the bus driver pulled into the zoo parking lot. The drive had gone by fast. Nobody had found the frog.

Mr. Daly stood up. "Welcome to the zoo," he said. "I want everyone to walk off the bus. Line up outside with your buddy."

"What about the frog?" George called.

Mr. Daly shrugged. "I guess we'll have to catch it on the way home," he said.

Nancy and Julia got off the bus together. Some of the kids were still peeking under the seats for the frog. Nancy had a funny feeling that they were wasting their time.

Julia and Nancy walked by Mr. Daly.

"How's your tummy feeling?" the teacher asked Julia.

"My tummy?" Julia asked. "Oh, right! It's fine." She smiled a big, happy smile.

Mr. Daly smiled back.

Nancy motioned for Mr. Daly to come closer. "Is there really a frog loose on the bus?" she whispered in his ear.

"Not really," Mr. Daly whispered back. "But don't tell Julia. At least, not until we get back to school."

Nancy laughed. "Don't worry," she said. "Your secret is safe with me."

When Nancy got home that afternoon, she took out her detective notebook. She opened it to "The Case of the Practical Jokes" and began to write.

> The zoo trip was fun! We saw the flamingos *and* the bats. But the best part was when Mr. Daly played a joke on us! Worrying about frogs helped Julia forget to be afraid. Maybe Mr. Daly isn't such an old meanie, after all.
>
> Case closed.

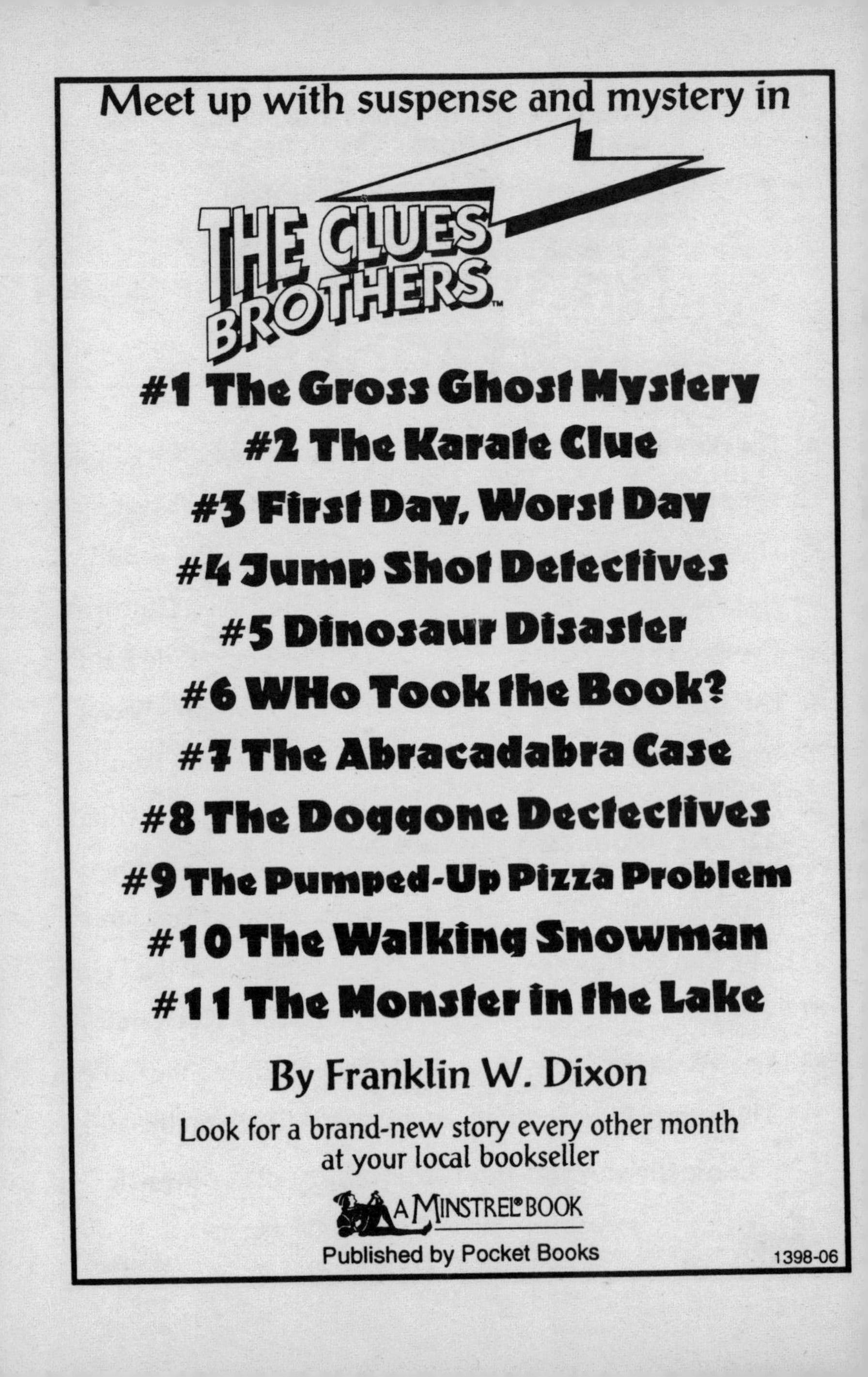

Meet up with suspense and mystery in
THE CLUES BROTHERS™
#1 The Gross Ghost Mystery
#2 The Karate Clue
#3 First Day, Worst Day
#4 Jump Shot Detectives
#5 Dinosaur Disaster
#6 Who Took the Book?
#7 The Abracadabra Case
#8 The Doggone Dectectives
#9 The Pumped-Up Pizza Problem
#10 The Walking Snowman
#11 The Monster in the Lake
By Franklin W. Dixon
Look for a brand-new story every other month
at your local bookseller
A MINSTREL® BOOK
Published by Pocket Books
1398-06